Dear Parent:

Congratulations! Your child is taking the first steps on an exciting journey. The destination? Independent reading!

STEP INTO READING® will help your child get there. The program offers five steps to reading success. Each step includes fun stories and colorful art. There are also Step into Reading Sticker Books, Step into Reading Math Readers, Step into Reading Phonics Readers, Step into Reading Write-In Readers, and Step into Reading Phonics Boxed Sets—a complete literacy program with something to interest every child.

Learning to Read, Step by Step!

Ready to Read   Preschool–Kindergarten
• big type and easy words • rhyme and rhythm • picture clues
For children who know the alphabet and are eager to begin reading.

Reading with Help   Preschool–Grade 1
• basic vocabulary • short sentences • simple stories
For children who recognize familiar words and sound out new words with help.

Reading on Your Own   Grades 1–3
• engaging characters • easy-to-follow plots • popular topics
For children who are ready to read on their own.

Reading Paragraphs   Grades 2–3
• challenging vocabulary • short paragraphs • exciting stories
For newly independent readers who read simple sentences with confidence.

Ready for Chapters   Grades 2–4
• chapters • longer paragraphs • full-color art
For children who want to take the plunge into chapter books but still like colorful pictures.

STEP INTO READING® is designed to give every child a successful reading experience. The grade levels are only guides. Children can progress through the steps at their own speed, developing confidence in their reading, no matter what their grade.

Remember, a lifetime love of reading starts with a single step!

Visit us on the Web!
StepIntoReading.com
www.randomhouse.com/kids

H9I4 4362 8/12

Educators and librarians, for a variety of teaching tools, visit us at
www.randomhouse.com/teachers

Library of Congress Cataloging-in-Publication Data
Hayward, Linda.
Baker, baker, cookie maker / by Linda Hayward ; illustrated by Tom Brannon. p. cm. — (Step into reading. A step 2 book)
Summary: Cookie Monster bakes beautiful and tempting cookies in his bakery, but he has so many customers that he cannot even have a taste.
ISBN 978-0-679-88379-1 (trade) — ISBN 978-0-679-98379-8 (lib. bdg.)
[1. Cookies—Fiction. 2. Baking—Fiction. 3. Stories in rhyme.]
I. Brannon, Tom, ill. II. Title. III. Series: Step into reading. Step 2 book.
PZ8.3.H33384 Bak 2003 [E]—dc21 2002013339

Printed in the United States of America 18 17 16 15 14 13

STEP INTO READING®
STEP 2

Baker, Baker, Cookie Maker

123
SESAME STREET

by Linda Hayward
illustrated by Tom Brannon

Random House 🏠 New York

Cookie Monster,
cookie eater,
mixes batter
with his beater,

4

drops the dough
onto the sheet,

bakes the cookies.
Good to eat!

He puts the cookies
on a plate,
takes a cookie . . .
Oops, too late!

Baker, baker,
cookie maker,
here comes a hungry
cookie taker!

COOKIES! COOKIES!

Monster treat.

Some for munchers,
some for crunchers,

none for the baker
on Sesame Street.

Cookie Monster,
cookie cutter,
makes a batch
with peanut butter,

cuts the cookies
out of dough,

puts them on the plate . . .

Oh, no!

Baker, baker,
cookie maker,
here comes another
cookie taker!

COOKIES! COOKIES!

Monster treat.

Some for hikers,
some for bikers,

none for the baker

on Sesame Street.

Cookie Monster,
cookie master,
makes more cookies
even faster.

He pats the cookies
nice and flat;
makes them,
bakes them.
Look at that!

Baker, baker,
cookie maker,
here come some *more*
cookie takers!

COOKIES! COOKIES!
Monster treat.

Some for hoppers,
some for moppers,

and *one* for the baker

on Sesame Street.